HappyJack
Publishing

HappyJack Publishing
P.O. Box 30363 • Middleburg Heights, Ohio 44130

Marschall, Jack P.

Woulda, Coulda, and Shoulda:
Three down and out characters learn it's never too late to
live your dreams no matter how simple or complex they may be.
They are challenged and motivated by The Voice / Jack P. Marschall.

ISBN 0-9729672-0-6

Printed in the United States by Cleveland Business Forms
Layout and Design by Digital Impressions, Inc.

For more information: HappyJackPubs.com

DEDICATION

This book is dedicated to those who helped me
realize my dreams with constructive criticism,
support, inspiration and the magic of love.
Thanks for believing in me.

To my loving wife Sharon,
my children Eric, Sarah, Adam,
Lauren, my family and friends.

To my best friend, teacher
and father, Peter A. Marschall.

They were the best of friends.
They were also each other's worst enemy.
They loved each other's misery.
They loved to hear each other complain.
They loved to feel sorry for themselves because
     as they put it, life isn't fair.
And maybe they're right.
Everything bad that happened seem to happen to
     Woulda, Coulda and Shoulda.
Or so they thought.
If only things were different.

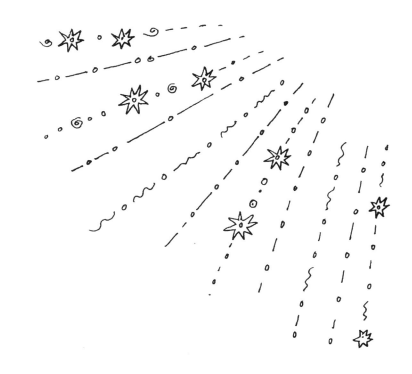

"Different how?" asked The Voice.

"What makes your life so tough compared to mine?"

"It's not my fault," said Woulda.

"And why is that?" asked The Voice.

"Because I didn't have control. If things were different I would have done this instead of that. I would have gone here instead of there. I would have said this instead of that.

I would have been so much better off, so much happier if I would have done things a little differently.

I would have been great. I would have been so popular.

I would have been a success."

"But you had all the chances in the world to do whatever you wanted," said The Voice. "It was your choice.
It was your life. It could have been so different. But who knows," The Voice added. "Maybe it's too late."

And The Voice smiled.

This made Woulda very angry and very sad.

She knew what The Voice said was true.

Still, Woulda wouldn't admit it.

She was never in a mood to accept responsibility.

She blamed everyone else for her problems.

And she was never, ever truly happy.

She looked around and always wanted what everybody else had.

"Actually, it's never too late," said The Voice.

"You can still change. You can still be whatever you want, whomever you want. It's all up to you."

Woulda just laughed at The Voice and went back with her two friends. They understood her. They agreed with everything Woulda said. But they also knew what The Voice said was true. Still, they were happy with their unhappiness. It was always someone else's fault.

And that's the way they liked it.

"Who do you think you are?" asked Coulda. "Life is a waste of time and nothing ever works out. Why do all the bad things happen to us? We're not to blame. We're the victims in this ugly life. We didn't do ANYTHING!"

"Now that I would agree with," said The Voice.
"And what do you mean by that?" yelled Coulda.
"It's pretty simple," said The Voice. "Way back when, you could have changed your life. You could have done this instead of that. You could have gone here instead of there.
You could have said this instead of that. You could have made different choices — made different decisions.
It could have changed your life," said The Voice.
"But you chose a different path."

"Oh yea," said Coulda.
"Changed my life for the better? It could have made me happy and rich and powerful! Is that what you're saying?"

"Oh no," said The Voice.
"It simply could have made you a different person. It could have made you stronger. It could have helped you appreciate the little things in life that others don't have — things that you take for granted," said The Voice.
"It could have been so different. But who knows," The Voice added, "maybe it's too late."

And The Voice smiled.

The conversation with The Voice made Coulda so angry he could barely breathe.

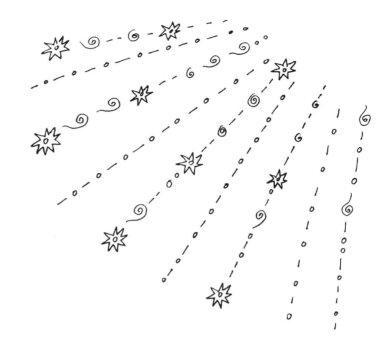

"Look here," he said. "I could have BEEN somebody — something special. I tried so hard to succeed, and if I wanted I could have gone all the way to the top. But I didn't want to. I could have been the best ever — in anything I chose. But I decided to do my own thing.
I didn't want to be like everybody else," Coulda said.
"And things never worked out like I planned. That's not my fault. It's so easy for everybody else. Why not for me?"

"Why NOT for you?" asked The Voice.
"Didn't you hear what you said about being special?" The Voice asked.
"You're special right now, just as you are. But you and your friends are still so unhappy, always regretting your choices and asking, 'what if?' If you don't like it then do whatever it takes to change. It could have been so different. But who knows," The Voice added. "Maybe it's too late."

And The Voice smiled.

Coulda and the others knew what The Voice said was true.
Still, they were happy with their unhappiness. It was always someone else's fault. And that's the way they liked it. "I could have been something special if I wanted," Coulda rambled on. "You should have seen me when I was young."

"Speaking of Shoulda," said The Voice, "where is he?"
"Oh I'm here," said Shoulda.

"I suppose you're going to start in on me now. Why don't you tell
        me about all the things I should have done in life but never did?"
"Why don't YOU?" asked The Voice.
"OK," said Shoulda.

"I admit, I should have taken control. I should have done this
        instead of that. I should have gone here instead of there. I
        should have said this instead of that."
"And?" asked The Voice.
"And I'm angry and sad that I didn't do what I wanted to do when I
        had the chance," said Shoulda. "There, now you have it. I
        should have done better. I should have known better. I
        should have tried harder. Maybe I should have taken more
        risks. We all could have tried something instead of nothing,"
        Shoulda added.

"What do you mean?" asked The Voice.
"I should have kept my dream alive instead of giving up," said
        Shoulda. I settled for less and I should have been true to
        myself. But it's too late now. It's too late for me. It's too late
        for Woulda. It's too late for Coulda. It could have been so
        different," said Shoulda.

And The Voice smiled.

"Why do you say that?" asked The Voice.
"Don't you know," The Voice said, "it's never too late."
"But you can never go back," said Shoulda. "It's too hard."

"That's the whole idea," said The Voice. "It's about the future and
    deciding what's to come."

There was silence.
Woulda, Coulda and Shoulda began to cry.
At first, they didn't know what to say.
Then they did what they knew best and said what they've been
    saying for so many years.

"Look," said Woulda, "we're happy being unhappy. We like to think
    of 'what if' all the time. And it's easy blaming others for the
    hand we were dealt. We made choices," Woulda added. "This
    is what we are and that's the way it is," said Coulda. "Is that
    so hard to understand?"
"Things can't be different," said Shoulda.
"It's too late."

"No," said The Voice. "You're not listening. "It's never too late."

"Easy for you to say," said Woulda
"Yea," said Coulda, "why don't you go away and bother somebody
    else?"
"Leave us alone," shouted Shoulda.

And then Shoulda said something very special.
"If you think we can change now, you're dreaming!"

The Voice paused and he smiled.

He took a deep breath and spoke these words.

"The dream is what it's all about. You haven't lost ANYTHING," he
said. "You're still the people you were many years ago. Sure,
you've changed — we all have.

But what's in your heart — the dream — is still there. It never goes
away. It fades and it flutters. It grows quiet and sometimes
hides. But it's always, always there, still beating and still waiting."

"Waiting for what?" laughed Woulda, Coulda and Shoulda.

"Waiting for you," said The Voice.

"What are you saying?" they shouted.

"The dream," said The Voice.

"It's what you wanted more than anything else. It's the person you
always wanted to be. It's the hope you had when you were
young. It's what is still in your heart — the magic that makes
it happen. Don't you remember?"

"Everybody has a dream," said Woulda, Coulda and Shoulda. "And
then things happen. You know, the dreams go away. Is that
so bad?" they asked.

"No," said The Voice. "Not if you're happy and content.

"Are you happy and content? Or do you go through life making
excuses about what you would have done or could have done
or should have done? You're not like that are you?" asked
The Voice.

And The Voice smiled.

"And you think it's easy chasing some stupid dream?" asked
Woulda, Coulda and Shoulda.

"I didn't say it was easy," said The Voice. "And I sure didn't say it
was stupid.

"Life is a journey," said The Voice. "There are challenges and tests at every turn. If you don't know where you're heading, any road will take you there. But why take the trip if you don't have a dream — ANY dream?" asked The Voice. "It might just be a waste of time," he said with a smile. "You do have a dream, don't you?" asked The Voice. "Well, yea," mumbled Woulda, Coulda and Shoulda. "Then why don't you start today?" asked The Voice.

"Start right now, this very minute. We're not going to be around here forever, you know."

There was a long pause.
The Voice even thought he heard some whimpering.
There was silence. And then Woulda, Coulda and Shoulda said something very special.

"What happens if we fail?"

"Then," said The Voice, "you can be proud that at least you tried. That in itself is an accomplishment. You'd be happy and satisfied knowing you gave it a shot. And you wouldn't be looking back anymore, living your life in the past. You'd be looking ahead for a chance at what COULD be — of what may actually become of your life."

"I may be old," said The Voice, "but I think that's more exciting than sitting around all day complaining and making excuses. And blaming others," said The Voice with a smile, "is a bad habit that IS older than me."

Woulda, Coulda and Shoulda began to think.

"If you're blessed with another tomorrow and a dream to last a lifetime," The Voice said, "then why not try? What do you have to lose — except your attitude?"

And The Voice smiled.

Woulda, Coulda and Shoulda couldn't speak.
They had tears in their eyes once again, knowing everything The
    Voice had said was true. They were sad about lost opportunities
    of the past. They were scared of the challenges and risks to
    come. But Woulda, Coulda and Shoulda surprised even
    themselves. They agreed there was absolutely nothing to lose.

To their amazement, they all remembered their hopes and their
    dreams from what seemed to be a lifetime ago. And for the
    first time in a long time, Woulda, Coulda and Shoulda were
    excited and happy. They were ready to start a journey that
    would change their lives forever.

They all said at the exact same time,
"If WE can do this, ANYBODY can."
The Voice was right, they thought. It's all about the dream.
And no, it's never too late.

And then, Woulda, Coulda and Shoulda wiped the tears from their
    eyes, looked at each other, they smiled and hugged.
For the first time they could remember they were truly happy, and
    for all the right reasons.

And The Voice smiled back.

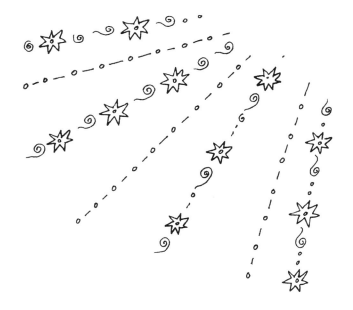

Have

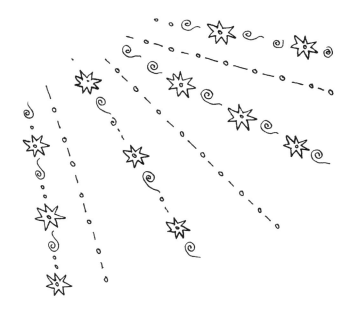

you

heard...

The Voice?

HappyJack
Publishing

HappyJack Publishing
P.O. Box 30363 • Middleburg Heights, Ohio 44130

Copyright © 2002 by Jack P. Marschall